A IS FOR AMOUR

A is for Amour, edited by Alison Tyler, is available from www.cleispress.com.

B

IS FOR BONDAGE

B is for Bondage, edited by Alison Tyler, is available from www.cleispress.com.

IS FOR CO-EDS

C is for Coeds, edited by Alison Tyler, is available from www.cleispress.com.

IS FOR DRESS-UP

D is for Dress-Up, edited by Alison Tyler, is available from www.cleispress.com.

E

IS FOR EXOTIC

E is for Exotic, edited by Alison Tyler, is available from www.cleispress.com.

IS FOR FETISH

F is for Fetish, edited by Alison Tyler, is available from www.cleispress.com.

G IS FOR GAMES

G is for Games, edited by Alison Tyler, is available from www.cleispress.com.

IS FOR HARDCORE

H is for Hardcore, edited by Alison Tyler, is available from www.cleispress.com.

IS FOR INDECENT

I is for Indecent, edited by Alison Tyler, is available from www.cleispress.com.

IS FOR JeaLOUSY

J is for Jealousy, edited by Alison Tyler, is available from www.cleispress.com.

IS FOR KINKY

K is for Kinky, edited by Alison Tyler, is available from www.cleispress.com.

L IS FOR LeaTHER

L is for Leather, edited by Alison Tyler, is available from www.cleispress.com.

IS FOR MASTER

M is for Master, edited by Alison Tyler, is available from www.cleispress.com.

N IS FOR NAUGHTY

N is for Naughty, edited by Alison Tyler, is available from www.cleispress.com.

IS FOR ORGASM

O is for Orgasm, edited by Alison Tyler, is available from www.cleispress.com.

IS FOR PERVERSE

P is for Perverse, edited by Alison Tyler, is available from www.cleispress.com.

IS FOR QUICKIE

Q is for Quickie, edited by Alison Tyler, is available from www.cleispress.com.

R

IS FOR RAUNCHY

R is for Raunchy, edited by Alison Tyler, is available from www.cleispress.com.

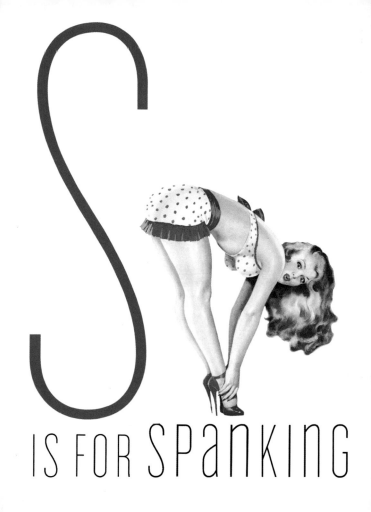

IS FOR Spanking

S is for Spanking, edited by Alison Tyler, is available from www.cleispress.com.

IS FOR TRASHY

T is for Trashy, edited by Alison Tyler, is available from www.cleispress.com.

IS FOR UNDERWEAR

U is for Underwear, edited by Alison Tyler, is available from www.cleispress. ⬤

IS FOR VOYEUR

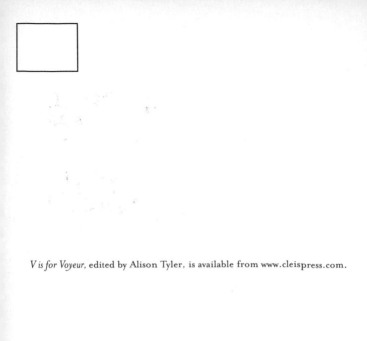

V is for Voyeur, edited by Alison Tyler, is available from www.cleispress.com.

W

IS FOR WICKED

W is for Wicked, edited by Alison Tyler, is available from www.cleispress.com.

IS FOR X-RATED

X is for X-Rated, edited by Alison Tyler, is available from **www.cleispress.com**.

IS FOR YEARNING

Y is for Yearning, edited by Alison Tyler, is available from www.cleispress.com.

IS FOR ZIPPER

Z is for Zipper, edited by Alison Tyler, is available from www.cleispress.com.